ZONE ⑬

Cyberspace
Warrior

David Orme

Text illustrations by Dave Bowyer
Cover illustration by Mark Duffin

First published in 1998 by
Stanley Thornes Publishers Ltd

Reprinted in 2001 by:
Nelson Thornes Ltd
Delta Place
27 Bath Road
CHELTENHAM
GL53 7TH
United Kingdom

03 \ 10 9 8 7 6 5

A catalogue record for this book is available from the British Library

ISBN 0-7487-3615-8

Typeset by Tech-Set Ltd.

Printed and bound in Great Britain by T.J. International Ltd.

CONTENTS

CYBERWORLD

Eddy Barnes stopped outside the door. CYBERWORLD, it said, in big letters. This was the place!

Eddy went in. A woman was sitting at a desk.

"Good morning," she said. "Welcome to Cyberworld!"

Cyberworld was the latest craze. You put on a special helmet. It linked up with your brain. You could visit all sorts of worlds and have adventures. It was just as if you were there.

The woman showed Eddy the programs he could choose.

"Cyberspace Warrior," said Eddy. "This looks good."

'Become a warrior in cyberspace,' it said. 'Defeat all the deadly enemies!'

There were pictures of some of the enemies. One looked like an alien with three heads. Another was a caveman with a big club of wood. The club had nails sticking out of it.

"That will be twenty pounds, please."

"Twenty pounds!" said Eddy. "What a rip off!"

He paid the money. He was taken into a small room. He sat in a chair.

"You can end the game at any time you want," said the woman. "All you have to do is shout out your password. Don't forget your password!"

She put the helmet on his head.

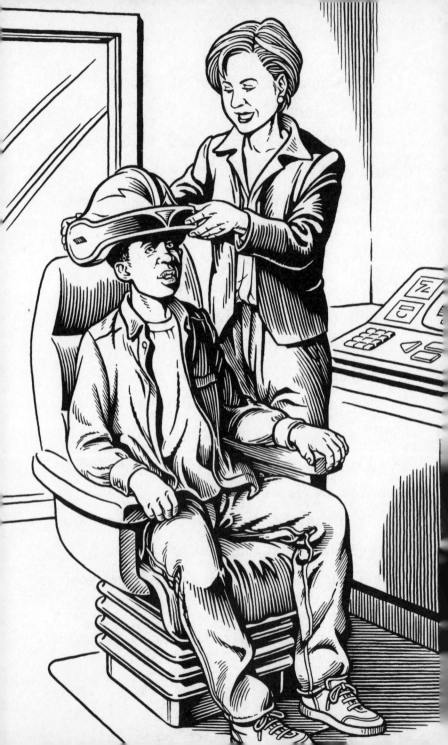

"What password would you like?"

"I know," said Eddy. "This place is a real rip off. I'll choose RIP OFF as my password!"

The woman laughed. She pressed a switch.

"GAME ON," said a voice.

THE GAME

STARTS

Eddy found himself sitting on a big rock. He looked round. What a terrible place! There was nothing growing there. There were huge rocks scattered about. The sun was very hot.

He looked down at himself. He was wearing a leather skirt. He had a heavy leather jacket. A sword hung at his side.

Eddy didn't feel brave any more. He knew he would have to fight with a terrible enemy. He was no good at fighting! He was a bit of a weed really. He didn't want to play any more.

Eddy knew that the game would stop if he shouted out the password. Now, what was that password again?

Suddenly there was a roar. A huge man jumped out from behind the rock. He was dressed like Eddy. He had a sword.

Eddy was very frightened. When Eddy got frightened, he forgot things.

Eddy forgot the password.

He jumped up and started to run.

"Come here, you coward!" yelled the big man. "Fight, you worm!"

Eddy was trying to remember the password. Perhaps it was what the other kids called him at school.

"Stupid weed!" he shouted.

This wasn't the password. But it made the big man very angry.

"What did you call me?" he yelled. "Just you wait till I get you!"

Eddy tried to hide behind a rock. The big man saw him. Eddy was trapped!

"I'll chop you into little pieces!" roared the big man. "Now, which bit shall I chop off first?"

The huge sword started to chop. Suddenly, the big man disappeared. Eddy heard a voice.

"Round one is over. You lost. Get ready for round two!"

Eddy groaned. If only he could remember the password!

THE NEXT

ROUND

Eddy was on an alien planet. There were three moons in the sky. He was in a forest of funny-looking trees. He was standing in an open part of the forest. He decided to hide in the trees. He remembered the alien in the picture. It had three heads! You would have to shoot all the heads to kill the alien.

He was wearing a spacesuit this time. He checked for weapons. That must be a ray gun!

Eddy felt something tickling the back of his neck. He turned round.

Giant spiders! They were hanging down from the trees. They had huge webs. Eddy hated spiders. He fired the gun at them. Zap! Zap! Zap!

Eddy was a bad shot. At last, all the spiders were dead.

There was a roaring noise behind him. Eddy groaned. 'Why do all the enemies have to roar?' he wondered.

The three-headed alien was coming through the trees! It had a long slimy body and very short legs.

"Die, Earthman, die!" roared the alien.

Eddy aimed the gun. 'This ought to be easy!' he thought. He pulled the trigger.

Nothing happened.

He had used up the weapon on the spiders!

"Die, Earthman, die!" said all three heads at once.

"Can't we talk about this?" said Eddy.

If only he could remember the password!

He suddenly remembered the rude name he used for his little sister. Perhaps that was it!

"Slug face!" he yelled.

The alien heads screamed in rage.

"No one calls us slug face!" they yelled. "Get ready to die! We will eat you alive! Now which bit shall we eat first?"

The heads each chose a bit of Eddy to eat first. The teeth started to munch. . .

"Round two is over. You lost. Get ready for round three!"

Whatever was that password?

TENTACLES OF

DOOM!

Eddy found himself at the bottom of the sea. It was quite dark. He was wearing a mask. He had air tanks on his back.

Eddy didn't like it here. He thought he would swim to the surface.

Then he remembered he couldn't swim.

He tried kicking his legs. He didn't seem to be getting anywhere. He wondered what the enemy could be. He thought about great white

sharks. He hoped it wasn't that. There was only one thing worse than a great white shark. That was. . .

A giant octopus!

Eddy knew the octopus was there when a tentacle grabbed his leg.

What weapon did he have? He reached down to his belt.

A knife! Good!

He looked at the knife. It was a bit small! Not so good!

More tentacles grabbed Eddy. What was that password? It was something to do with how much money he had paid.

If only he hadn't gone to Cyberworld! Eddy was a real sucker!

'That's it!' thought Eddy

"Sucker!" he shouted.

"Oh yes!" said the octopus. "I forgot the suckers!"

Suckers appeared on the tentacles. They held him tightly. Eddy couldn't reach the knife.

Suddenly, Eddy couldn't breathe. The octopus had pulled off his air tanks with its suckers!

Eddy struggled. Everything started to go black.

"Round three is over. You lost. Prepare for round four!"

Whatever was that password?

THE MUTANT

KILLER ROBOT

Eddy was standing in a huge city. It looked very modern. He was wearing a silver uniform.

A voice spoke in his ear.

"Calling all cops! Calling all cops! Mutant killer robot on the loose! Heading for street 29!"

Eddy looked at a sign on the wall. He could have guessed.

The sign said: Street 29.

The mutant killer robot marched up the

street. It had big glass eyes. They looked at Eddy.

"You are a cop," said the robot. "Cops are the enemies of the robots! Get ready. . ."

"Yes, I know," said Eddy. "Get ready to die!"

"How did you know I was going to say that?"

"Just a lucky guess," said Eddy.

Eddy was getting cross now. He wanted to get out of the stupid game. He still couldn't remember the password. He tried to get past the robot. The robot grabbed him with a metal arm.

Eddy didn't often lose his temper. But now he was really angry.

"Let go of me, you stupid tin can!" he yelled. "Or I'll RIP OFF your arm!"

Suddenly the robot was gone. The city was gone as well. Eddy found himself back at Cyberworld.

"GAME OVER," said the voice.

"You got to level four!" said the woman. "You must be really tough! Most people give up when they see the octopus!"

Eddy felt really proud. Really tough!

"Did you enjoy it?" said the woman.

"It was great! As soon as I've saved another twenty pounds, I'll be back!"